There's an Elephant in the Garage

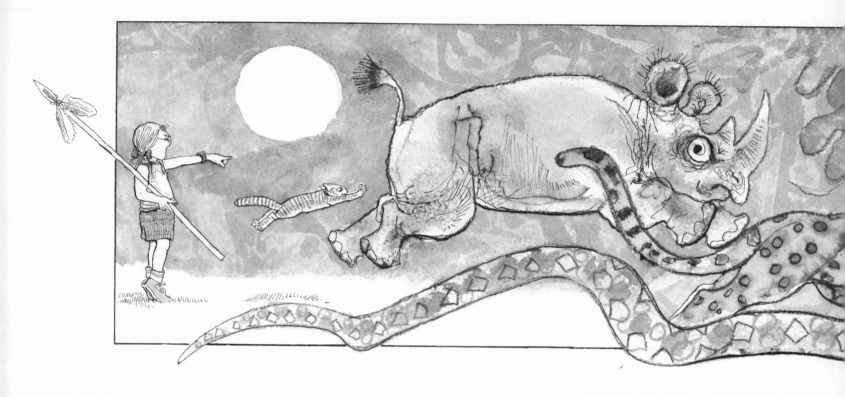

There's a

Elephant in the Garage

by Douglas F. Davis
illustrated by Steven Kellogg

E. P. Dutton   New York

Library of Congress Cataloging in Publication Data

Davis, Douglas F.   There's an elephant in the garage.

SUMMARY: The adventures of a little girl and her cat
as they hunt rogue elephants in the family garage.
[1. Cats—Fiction]   I. Kellogg, Steven.   II. Title.
PZ7.D28594Th   1979   [E]   79-11378   ISBN: 0-525-41050-3

Published in the United States by E. P. Dutton, a Division
of Elsevier-Dutton Publishing Company, Inc., New York
Published simultaneously in Canada by Clarke,
Irwin & Company Limited, Toronto and Vancouver
Editor: Ann Durell   Designer: Meri Shardin

Printed in the U.S.A.   First Edition
10 9 8 7 6 5 4 3 2 1

For Rema
D. D.

To Laurie with love
S. K.

One afternoon when April Janice Jones taught
Zelda to hunt the fierce African rhinoceros, and
Zelda did THIS to the deliveryman in the kitchen,
her mother said, "April Janice Jones! Get THAT
CAT out of the house THIS INSTANT!"

"She can sleep in the garage until she learns
some manners!"

"But, mother—" protested April Janice Jones.

Her mother pretended to be deaf.

That night April Janice Jones carried Zelda's
bed and Zelda and a bag of cookies and a flashlight into the dark garage. "We're running away
to Africa," she told Zelda.

"We'll hunt elephants big as houses. But for something THAT dangerous we'll need brave friends along—like bears. Those will do."

Two great growling bears rumbled toward them.
"STOP!" commanded April Janice Jones. "Zelda
and I are going on an elephant hunt. Want to
come?"

Amazed, the bears stopped in their tracks. After much nervous rumbling and grumbling, they decided they would go.

"Don't worry," said April Janice Jones. "Zelda and I will protect you. Let's get started."

The hunt began.

They crept deeper and deeper into the wild
jungle. Even the bears were nervous at first—
until they saw how bravely April and Zelda led
the hunt.

And when they sighted a herd of fierce wild elephants, the bears were prepared to charge—behind April and Zelda of course.

"STOP!" commanded April Janice Jones. "It's time for lunch."

They sat in a circle eating cookies, in a jungle
clearing tangled all around with vines and mon-
keys and enormous trees.

Suddenly they heard loud crunching footsteps.

April Janice Jones and Zelda crept out to have
a look, followed by the two big bears.

They saw a HUGE rogue elephant with long
pointed tusks and wild red eyes.
"Surround him," April told the bears.

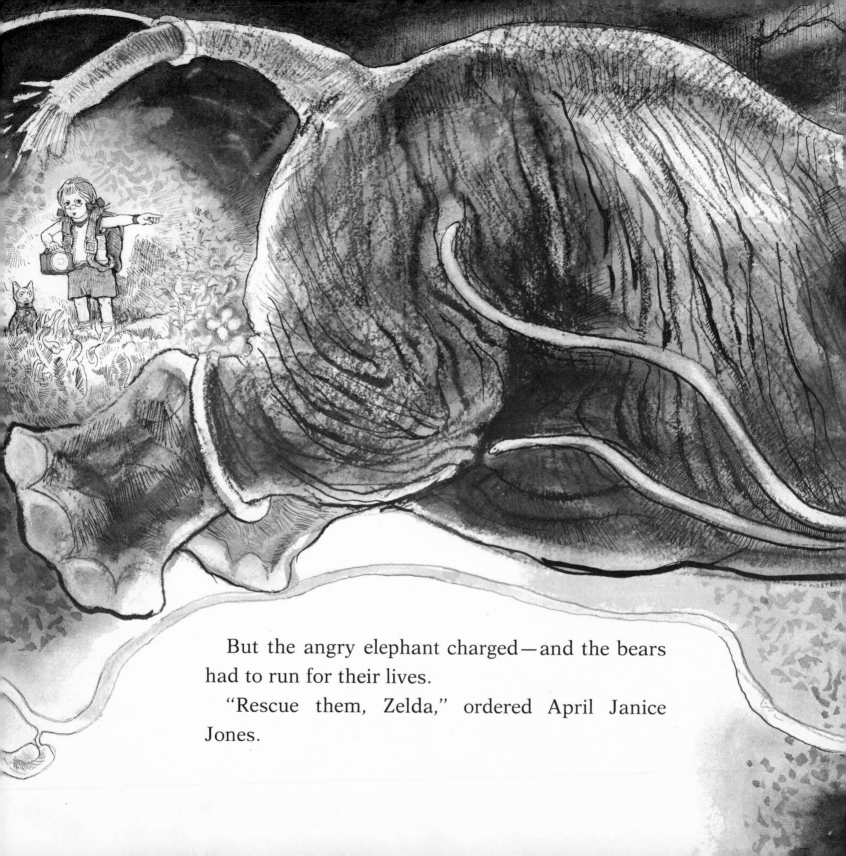

But the angry elephant charged—and the bears
had to run for their lives.

"Rescue them, Zelda," ordered April Janice
Jones.

And Zelda did THIS to the terrible rogue elephant thundering toward them—and he stopped, shuddering in his tracks.

April Janice Jones looked straight into his wild red eyes and said, "Until you learn some manners, you'll have to sleep in the garage."

"Come, Zelda."

When she had thanked the bears for coming along on the hunt, April Janice Jones carried Zelda's bed and Zelda and the rest of the cookies and the flashlight back into the house.

"There's an elephant in the garage," April Janice
Jones told her mother. "So Zelda will have to stay
in the house tonight—to protect you and father.
And besides—she's learned some manners."